TEEN GUIDE TO SOCIAL & EMOTIONAL SKILLS

DEVELOPING
RELATIONSHIP SKILLS

by Tammy Gagne

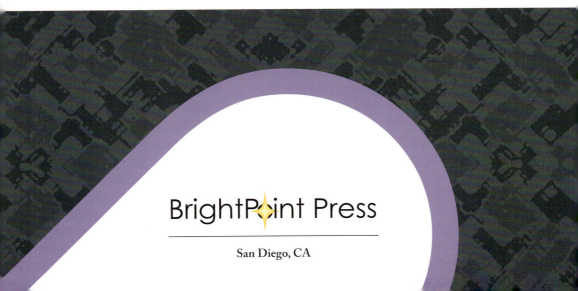

BrightPoint Press

San Diego, CA

BrightPoint Press

© 2023 BrightPoint Press
an imprint of ReferencePoint Press, Inc.
Printed in the United States

For more information, contact:
BrightPoint Press
PO Box 27779
San Diego, CA 92198
www.BrightPointPress.com

ALL RIGHTS RESERVED.

No part of this work covered by the copyright hereon may be reproduced or used in any form or by any means—graphic, electronic, or mechanical, including photocopying, recording, taping, web distribution, or information storage retrieval systems—without the written permission of the publisher.

LIBRARY OF CONGRESS CATALOGING-IN-PUBLICATION DATA

Names: Gagne, Tammy, author.
Title: Developing relationship skills / by Tammy Gagne.
Description: San Diego, CA: BrightPoint Press, [2023] | Series: Teen guide to social & emotional skills | Includes bibliographical references and index. | Audience: Grades 10-12
Identifiers: LCCN 2022008627 (print) | LCCN 2022008628 (eBook) | ISBN 9781678204341 (hardcover) | ISBN 9781678204358 (eBook)
Subjects: LCSH: Interpersonal relations in adolescence--Juvenile literature. | Interpersonal relations--Juvenile literature.
Classification: LCC BF724.3.I58 G34 2023 (print) | LCC BF724.3.I58 (eBook) | DDC 158.20835--dc23/eng/20220304
LC record available at https://lccn.loc.gov/2022008627
LC eBook record available at https://lccn.loc.gov/2022008628

CONTENTS

AT A GLANCE   4

INTRODUCTION   6
SEEKING AND OFFERING HELP

CHAPTER ONE   12
RELATIONSHIP SKILLS AT SCHOOL

CHAPTER TWO   28
RELATIONSHIP SKILLS AT HOME

CHAPTER THREE   44
RELATIONSHIP SKILLS WITH FRIENDS

CHAPTER FOUR   60
RELATIONSHIP SKILLS IN THE COMMUNITY

Glossary   74
Source Notes   75
For Further Research   76
Index   78
Image Credits   79
About the Author   80

AT A GLANCE

- Developing relationships skills at school often involves teamwork. Learning to work well with others helps students form positive relationships as they achieve academic goals.

- Many classmates become friends. Social and emotional learning helps young people develop the skills to manage these relationships.

- Working on communication with family members is a great way to practice relationship skills.

- Listening to others is an important part of building relationship skills.

- Developing relationship skills can help people make new friends.

- Offering help to someone who needs it is a great way to build relationship skills.

- Standing up for others who are being wronged is a good way to promote social and emotional learning in one's community.

- Practicing cultural humility helps everyone feel a sense of equity. This too is an important part of developing relationship skills.

INTRODUCTION

SEEKING AND OFFERING HELP

Jackson loved being the captain of his baseball team. But he disliked dealing with difficult situations like this one. Ethan had been striking out a lot lately. Some of the players teased him. Others blamed him for losses. Jackson knew he had to do something to help his teammate. But he

Good team captains are aware of the issues in a team and seek to find solutions.

needed some guidance. He decided to ask his coach for advice.

"I'm glad you came to me with this," Coach Morgan said. "Let's brainstorm ideas about what we can do."

Seeking advice from a coach or mentor can help lead to a team's success.

"Well," Jackson began, "I saw Ethan's face the last time he struck out. He looked embarrassed and frustrated. He probably feels like he is letting everyone down. Maybe he could focus on his batting better if he felt more support from the team. I'd like to talk to everyone before practice tomorrow. I want to say how important it is to be positive with one another. Teasing is mean and unhelpful. It needs to stop."

"I think that is a great approach," Coach Morgan said. "Let's also focus the practice on batting. We have a great outfield. But everyone could use more batting practice. Let's encourage everyone to work on it together. A group effort might also help Ethan feel less singled out."

Jackson felt better now that a plan was in place.

Effective leaders value every person on the team.

"You're a good captain," Coach Morgan added. "Standing up for others is a big part of being an effective leader."

WHAT ARE RELATIONSHIP SKILLS?

Jackson used relationship skills to work through his problem. Relationship skills are a part of social and emotional learning

(SEL). First, he put himself in his teammate's shoes. He shared his feelings with his coach. Together, they came up with a strategy to solve the problem.

Relationship skills focus on having **empathy** for other people's emotions. It requires a person to look at situations from others' viewpoints. Relationship skills can help people form positive relationships, achieve goals, and resolve conflicts. These skills can be used at home, in school, with friends, and in one's community.

CHAPTER ONE

RELATIONSHIP SKILLS AT SCHOOL

Jackson's English teacher had divided the students into pairs to write a one-act play. Jackson was excited about the assignment. But he was also nervous. He knew it would count for a big part of his grade. He was also frustrated with his partner, Emma. He thought girls were

Group projects can be frustrating if there is not good communication.

supposed to be good at writing. But all Emma wanted to do was talk about other things.

    Jackson almost snapped at her when she started talking about their school's art show. Instead, he took a breath and remembered something he had learned recently. His health class was studying relationship skills. One of the things the teacher focused on was resolving conflicts constructively. He tried to think of a way to bring the subject back to the play. He knew that Emma had several paintings in the art show.

"I have an idea," he shared. "How about we make the main character an artist who restores famous paintings? There could be a big heist at the museum he works at."

"That's a great idea," Emma replied. She then confided, "You are a lot better at this

Talking about the other person's interests can be helpful in conversation.

than I am. I find painting so much easier than writing." At this moment, Jackson recalled another important step in building relationship skills. His health teacher said people should always resist **stereotypes**. He realized he should not have assumed that Emma was good at writing because she is a girl. "Hey," she added. "Let's also make the main character a woman." Jackson nodded and smiled. He felt like they were finally working together.

DEVELOPING RELATIONSHIP SKILLS AT SCHOOL

Teamwork is a primary way students can build relationship skills at school. Cooperating with others makes group tasks easier and more fun. It also lessens arguing and frustration. Some group assignments require problem solving. Students are more

Teamwork not only helps people finish tasks faster, but it also helps build character.

likely to succeed at finding the answers by working as a team.

Approaching relationships with a positive attitude makes a big difference in the classroom. Each person has something of value to offer. Keeping this in mind helps create an open and positive learning environment. Everyone's contribution can be heard and appreciated. Danny Wagner of Common Sense Education says, "If we're lucky, students will take that learning outside the classroom and **rally** behind their peers to make the world a better place for us all."[1]

Another part of developing relationship skills involves practicing cultural humility. This means respecting the cultures of others while being humble about one's own. School is a setting where many types of

At school, people may meet students and teachers of different cultures and backgrounds.

people work together. Students, teachers, and other faculty members may come from a variety of different cultures.

Students and teachers may belong to vastly different generations. Their ethnicities and religions may also be different.

These differences can lead to diverse opinions on matters of everyday life. Many people dress differently, listen to different music, and eat different foods. Remaining

> **FINDING COMMON GROUND**
>
> Learning relationship skills can bring people together in ways they don't expect. A great example can be found in the book *Freedom Writers*, which was also turned into a movie. In it, a teacher has a classroom of students from very different backgrounds. She asks them all to start keeping journals and sharing the entries as they feel comfortable. Through this process, the students learn that they actually have far more in common than they ever imagined they would.

humble and flexible when it comes to the beliefs and practices of others helps people get along better.

HOW DEVELOPING RELATIONSHIP SKILLS CAN HELP STUDENTS LEARN

Building relationship skills can improve a student's academic success. Asking for help can be hard sometimes. A person struggling with school may feel embarrassed. He may worry about what others think. But learning when and how to ask for help when needed is the best way to get it.

Sometimes reaching out to fellow students can help. Study groups can be especially helpful when reviewing material. Other times a teacher's help may be needed. For example, some teachers offer to work with students after class. If a lot of help is needed, finding a tutor might be more useful.

Students who struggle with expressing themselves in a healthy way can also benefit from developing their relationship skills. These skills can help these students deal with difficult feelings such as frustration. Students are less likely to disrupt class

Students can ask their teachers for help if they are confused about an assignment.

when they learn how to manage frustration better. For example, a student who fears public speaking may feel frustrated before an oral presentation. She may act out while others are delivering presentations for this reason. Talking about her fear and frustration to a teacher or classmate ahead of time can help her identify the cause of the problem. Volunteering to go first might help her to listen better when her classmates present.

Expressing one's frustration can be a great way to lessen it. But it should be done

> **RELATIONSHIP SKILLS CAN PREVENT BULLYING**
>
> Empathy is one of the most useful social and emotional skills for relationships. It involves looking at situations from others' viewpoints. Students can also work on paying more attention to body language and tone of voice. Both offer clues to how a person is feeling. Students who use empathy are more likely to respect and include other students. This can lead to more healthy relationships with friends and can help lessen bullying.

in a healthy way in the classroom. When people stay focused on learning, academic goals are easier to achieve.

Teachers who help students build relationship skills create environments where academic learning is easier. These teachers may take extra time to get to know their students. They might also stay after school to offer extra help. Erin Walsh is an educator who teaches people about social and emotional learning. She points out that building relationship skills works best when everyone works together. She also wants people to know that this can take time. She says, "This work can be difficult and can't be solved in one session or one program—it's about **sustained** work over time."[2]

Developing relationship skills can also help young people make friends and manage those relationships. At first this may mean simply learning how to start conversations with others. Later, it may mean learning how to listen to others better. Students attend school to learn. But they can also make valuable friendships during the process. Classmates become enjoyable companions in learning. They can

Students can build relationship skills when they participate in extracurricular activities like orchestra or band.

also be great sources of support. Chatting while eating lunch, studying together after school, or enjoying recreational time away from schoolwork all add to a person's educational experience.

CHAPTER TWO

RELATIONSHIP SKILLS AT HOME

"If I find your socks on the floor again, I'm going to throw them away!" Jackson had just walked into the room he shared with his older brother Jayden. He hadn't even set his backpack down. And already Jayden was yelling at him.

Arguments between siblings tend to happen often. However, there are ways conflict can be handled in a healthy manner.

"That's not fair," Jackson replied. "You have no right to get rid of my things."

"It's also not fair of you to leave your stinky socks on the floor. They belong in the hamper or a toxic waste facility." It wasn't a new argument. Jayden was a neat freak. He liked everything put away and in its place. Jackson wasn't as good about picking up after himself.

Jayden's comment made Jackson angry. He wanted to yell back. But he knew that more arguing wouldn't help. Instead, he decided to take a deep breath and respond more calmly.

"I'm sorry," Jackson began. "I know it bothers you when I leave stuff lying around. I'll try to be better about it if you can try to be more patient with me when I mess up." He knew that they both needed to work on

Speaking calmly can help ease tension in an argument between siblings.

communicating with each other better. "I really will try," he added.

Jayden was still annoyed. But he too was able to calm down. He could tell that Jackson was finally taking the problem seriously. "I didn't mean to yell," he said. "I just feel like you don't listen to me. I won't throw them away. But can you at least not leave them on my side of the room? I have to do homework in here. And, you know, breathe." Jayden smiled to let his brother know he was no longer angry. Jackson smiled back. He had used his relationship skills to stop the argument.

GETTING AND GIVING SUPPORT AT HOME

Asking for support isn't always easy. Some people find it difficult to admit to others when they are going through a tough time.

Healthy families communicate with each other.

Knowing how and when to offer support can also be challenging sometimes. But family members who are healthy communicators can be excellent sources of support for one another.

Working on relationships at home is a great way to build good relationship skills in general. Professors Jodi Dworkin and Joyce Serido study education and relationships at the University of Minnesota. They wrote, "The family is a training ground for exploring feelings and being in relationships."[3] There are many types of families in the world today. Likewise, there are many ways they can support one another. But most strategies can be adapted to work for families who have a willingness to learn.

Families can support each other by keeping the lines of communication open.

Seeking help from a family therapist can improve interactions between family members.

For instance, they may start each day by checking in with one another. Asking parents, siblings, or other household members how they are feeling each morning is a great way to do this. This type of daily check-in provides a great opportunity to discuss problems. Asking people how they are doing also lets them know that others care.

Sometimes all people need is someone to listen to them. Talking about a problem

THE IMPORTANCE OF LISTENING

Family members can show they care about one another by expressing their own thoughts and feelings. But they also need to listen to their loved ones. The best listeners make eye contact with the person who is speaking. This helps show that they are paying attention. They also make a point of not interrupting the speaker. People feel better about communicating when they feel heard. Good listening skills also increase understanding of what is being said.

with a trusted family member can make it easier to find a solution. When families talk often, it can also be easier to ask for support when it is needed.

RESOLVING CONFLICTS CONSTRUCTIVELY

Learning to resolve conflicts constructively is an important step in building relationship skills. Every family experiences arguments. But it is how they deal with it that matters most.

The first thing to remember when a conflict occurs is that problems are harder to solve when negative emotions are strong.

A good way to measure these feelings is by comparing them to traffic light colors. A person who is feeling red is angry. This person needs to stop and take a break to calm down before trying to discuss the problem. Feeling yellow isn't as intense as red. But a person feeling yellow may not be ready to communicate appropriately. Someone feeling green is ready to listen and respond constructively.

Once everyone is calm enough to talk, the next step is to identify the problem. Stating the conflict clearly is a good way to make sure that everyone involved

When people are in an argument, it is difficult to speak and listen attentively. Stopping and taking a break can help people calm their anger.

understands what the issue is. Once the problem is identified, family members can share ideas for how to best solve the problem. They can then decide on a solution together.

The Child Mind Institute's Juliann Garey says, "Of course, the tricky thing here is that it's usually hard to know what the best option really is. And that's okay!"[4] She points out that the family's goal should be making their best effort at solving the problem. The first solution doesn't have to work perfectly.

OTHER SITUATIONS IN WHICH SEL HELPS

Being part of a family comes with ups and downs. Living with other people can be hard sometimes. Developing relationship skills can help family members get through even some of the toughest challenges.

Teens do not always like the household rules their parents make for them. For

If a person disagrees with a parent's household rule, he or she can try to talk to the parent to find a better solution.

example, curfews and limits on screen time can be frustrating sometimes. Learning how to talk about the rules in appropriate ways can help everyone deal with this problem. Discussing the situation respectfully makes it easier to find fair solutions.

Building relationship skills can even help a family communicate when dealing with

Although a family may not find a perfect solution, working together to solve the problem is what matters the most.

bigger problems, such as divorce or a death in the family. These are some of the most difficult situations a parent or a child can face. Working on relationship skills can help everyone as they move through tough life challenges. Two of the most important skills in these situations are expressing one's feelings and listening to others. Each person may experience the loss differently. But communication and empathy can help each family member better understand what the others are going through.

BOX BREATHING

Breathing exercises can help a person facing a stressful situation with a family member. One technique is called box breathing. The person feeling stressed begins by breathing in while counting to four. The next step is holding the breath for another count of four. Another count of four is used to let the breath out through the mouth. These steps can be repeated as many times as needed. Box breathing helps many people feel more relaxed and in control.

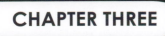

RELATIONSHIP SKILLS WITH FRIENDS

On his way to math class, Jackson saw a girl walking ahead of him. Her eyes kept moving from a piece of paper to the room numbers above the classroom doors. She looked lost. She also looked different from most of the other students. She wore a **hijab** over her hair.

At school, people can help new students adjust to their surroundings.

Jackson thought she might be the new exchange student he'd heard was coming. But he wasn't sure what to do. He wanted to offer his help. But he wasn't sure if the girl spoke English. He also didn't know if she wanted his help.

Seeing the girl reminded Jackson of his first day at this school. He remembered how hard it was to be the new kid. Luckily, a girl named Lily had helped him find his way on his first day. He was still grateful to her for offering her help. He was a lot shyer then. He and Lily remained friends to this day. He decided to take the same chance that Lily had taken with him.

"Hi," he said. "I'm Jackson. Are you looking for Mrs. Platz's math class?"

People can practice their relationship skills by introducing themselves to others.

"Yes!" the girl answered with a relieved smile. She then added, "I am Amira."

"This is the right place," Jackson replied. "You will like Mrs. P," he went on. "She's a great teacher. She always lets us out a few minutes early for lunch too. By the way, my friends and I sit at the big table by the door. You can eat with us today if you want."

"I would like that," Amira said. She spoke a bit more slowly than Jackson did. But her English was excellent. She seemed nice too. He was glad he had spoken up. Maybe he had just made a new friend.

THE IMPORTANCE OF BEING POSITIVE AND SUPPORTIVE

Making negative assumptions about others isn't helpful. It can be easy to fill in the blanks with worries and fears. Jackson worried that Amira might not be

Judging others based on their appearance can lead to bullying.

friendly. He also feared that he wouldn't be able to communicate well with her due to a language barrier. But neither of these things turned out to be the case. He also was reminded that wearing a

Interacting with different types of people can change one's prejudices.

hijab didn't mean that Amira was from a non-English-speaking country. Hijabs are part of the Muslim faith, which anyone can practice. An important relationship skill is avoiding assumptions about others.

Learning about prejudice toward people with different religions or ethnicities is also important.

Most people worry about bad outcomes when speaking to others. No one wants to say or do the wrong thing. No one wants to be rejected either. But assuming the worst in a person can make a situation bad when it isn't.

Offering help to someone who needs it is a great way to form a positive relationship. But it can be scary to reach out to a stranger. Jackson worried that Amira wouldn't want his help. But then he remembered how much Lily's help had meant to him when he needed it. It wasn't as scary when he thought about it from a new student's perspective.

MAKING NEW FRIENDS

Making and keeping friends are important in life. Many activities are more fun when done with other people. Friends make people feel less lonely. Having friends helps a person build self-confidence and self-esteem. Friends can help people feel like they belong. Studies have even found that having friends reduces bullying. Bullies

Relationship skills are important when creating and maintaining friendships.

are less likely to pick on someone who has the support of others.

Some people seem to make new friends with hardly any effort. Others have a harder time with this process. Relationship skills can make it easier. Many of the

Having a common interest helps make great friendships.

same behaviors one uses with current friends can also be used to make new ones. Being kind, showing empathy, and asking questions are all great starts to a new friendship.

Common interests often bring people together. Sharing an interest in sports or music is a great conversation starter. Many times, people are drawn to others who are a lot like them. But this isn't the only way to find great friends. Vincent Iannelli is a pediatrician and author. He explains, "There is so much that kids can learn from people that they might not expect to have as much in common with."[5]

DEVELOPING RELATIONSHIP SKILLS WITH FRIENDS

Building relationship skills doesn't just help when encountering strangers. It is also useful for people who already know each other. Effective communication is an important tool in any friendship. Misunderstandings can happen quickly when friends do not communicate clearly.

A LIFELONG SKILL

Making friends isn't just something people do when they are young. Creating friendships is a lifelong activity. Some friends remain close for years while others drift apart over time. This makes it even more important for people to keep making new friends. Even people with a solid friend group can benefit from spending time with new people. Bringing new friends into one's social circle can expand a person's knowledge, viewpoints, and happiness.

Relationship skills include communicating feelings effectively.

This makes it more difficult to move past conflicts when they come up.

Taking responsibility for one's actions is also a big part of good communication and problem solving. This can take practice. But the work is worth the effort. Michelle Garcia Winner helps people develop good social and emotional skills. She says, "Keeping a friend often involves learning to apologize." She adds, "It also means there will be some really special moments together."[6]

Communication isn't just about words. When two people speak to each other, it is called verbal communication. But feelings and ideas can be expressed in nonverbal ways too. Body language, facial expressions, and gestures can communicate a lot. A smile sends a very different message than a scowl.

Communication isn't even just about what a person is saying. It is also about listening and paying attention to others.

> **LOOKING AT THINGS DIFFERENTLY**
>
> One of the most valuable relationship skills is looking at situations from others' perspectives. There are at least two sides to every story. When people realize this, they become more open to seeing a situation from a viewpoint other than their own. People should never assume that others' experiences are the same as their own. Instead, they can use their imaginations to consider other points of view. Doing this can also help identify solutions that work for everyone.

CHAPTER FOUR

RELATIONSHIP SKILLS IN THE COMMUNITY

Jackson was walking home with his friends when they heard shouts and cheers. Something was clearly happening on Main Street. As they turned the corner, they saw people marching. Some of them were waving rainbow flags. Others held

Practicing relationship skills includes demonstrating compassion for people who don't have much representation.

signs. One read, "Love is love." Jackson knew instantly it was a gay pride parade.

"Oh no," Connor said when he realized what was happening. "It's one of *those*

People can resist negative social pressure, even among friend groups. This keeps friends accountable for their words and actions.

parades," he said, rolling his eyes. "Why don't you go home and knit some rainbow sweaters?" he shouted. Some of the boys walking with Jackson and Connor laughed. Others looked shocked by Connor's behavior. But they didn't say anything.

Jackson spoke up. "What is so bad about being gay?" he asked.

"Why?" Connor replied. "Are you gay?" He said it in an obnoxious singsong voice.

"No," Jackson answered. "But my older brother is. He just came out a few weeks ago. Now I understand why he was so scared that people would make fun of him." Connor was obviously uncomfortable now. But he didn't know what to say.

Another boy in the group then decided to speak up. "My aunt is gay too," Evan shared. "She had to get five stitches after she marched in a gay pride parade last year. A guy on the street threw a bottle at her."

"That's terrible," Connor said. Now he was the one who was shocked. "I would never do anything like that."

THE TREVOR PROJECT

Lesbian, gay, bisexual, transgender, or queer young people are four times more likely to attempt suicide than others. The Trevor Project is a nonprofit organization that aims to prevent these unnecessary deaths. It provides support for LGBTQ youth in numerous ways. Counselors are available at all times to assist young people who are struggling with their identity, coming out, or depression. The Trevor Project also works to educate others so they can become allies.

"I hope not," Jackson said. "But sometimes words and dirty looks can hurt just as much."

"I'm sorry," Connor said. "I had no idea your brother was gay. He's a cool guy. What can I do to make it right with you?"

"You can be an **ally**," Jackson said. He then explained, "That means being kind and supportive of people who identify as LGBTQ."

STANDING UP FOR OTHERS

Some people make hateful comments to keep others silent. This is called negative social pressure. When Connor was acting mean, some of the other boys may have laughed because it was the easy thing to do. But relationship skills teach people not to give in to negative social pressure.

Treating others badly because of their sexual orientation, gender, or race is called discrimination. People can help end discrimination by not joining in it. They can speak up when discrimination is happening. Even when one person speaks up, it can make it easier for others to do so as well.

CULTURAL HUMILITY IN THE COMMUNITY

People in the United States represent a wide variety of cultures. Culture does not

Being a silent bystander when witnessing bullying or discrimination is a problem.

just apply to one's ethnicity or nation of origin. Most people belong to more than one culture. There is family culture, school culture, and even social culture. No culture is better than another. But sometimes people from one culture will judge others.

Social and emotional learning teaches people to practice cultural humility. This means not being prideful or arrogant about one's own culture. People who practice cultural humility are sensitive and open to learning more about other cultures.

One of the most important things to remember about cultural humility is that there is always more to learn. Danny Wagner explains, "This is when we recognize that we have **biases** and limitations to our knowledge regarding another's culture."[7] Even people with the best intentions can form hasty opinions

When one person speaks up about an issue, others can feel more comfortable to speak up.

about other cultures. The key to cultural humility is realizing that these opinions can often lead us to harmful stereotypes.

DEVELOPING RELATIONSHIP SKILLS IN COMMUNITIES

Not everyone learns about relationship skills at home or at school. In these cases, practicing them in the community becomes even more important. Cassandra Kiger runs a mentoring program that teaches relationship skills. She explains, "Many students report that they do not even feel like they 'fit' in the schools they attend, as they might not feel a sense of belonging, purpose, and empowerment in the educational system."[8] Becoming involved in one's community can help fill this void.

Volunteering is a great way to be involved in a community. People can practice their relationship skills while helping others. Common ways of volunteering include working in a soup kitchen or homeless shelter, tutoring students, or visiting nursing homes. But it isn't just the recipients who benefit from a volunteer's time and effort. The volunteer also ends up better for it.

RESPECTING DIFFERENT HOLIDAYS

Several major holidays take place at the end of each year. They include Christmas, Hanukkah, and Kwanzaa. A good way to practice cultural humility is respecting that not everyone celebrates the same holidays. One way to do this is by saying "Happy Holidays" instead of a more specific greeting unless one is certain a person celebrates a specific holiday. Another way is showing interest in other people's holidays. Learning about other cultures' holiday traditions can also be fun.

BENEFITS OF VOLUNTEERING IN A COMMUNITY

94% OF PEOPLE SAY THEIR MOOD IMPROVED

95% OF PEOPLE SAY VOLUNTEERING MAKES THEIR COMMUNITY A BETTER PLACE

78% OF PEOPLE SAY IT LOWERS THEIR STRESS

96% OF PEOPLE SAY IT ADDS TO THEIR SENSE OF PURPOSE IN LIFE

Source: "Volunteering: Why Doing Good Is Good for You," Happify, n.d. www.happify.com.

Volunteering allows a person to be surrounded by people of different age groups and backgrounds. Not only do people practice their relationship skills through volunteering, but studies have also shown that they can increase their overall happiness.

Volunteering can help people make new friends. It also helps build volunteers' self-confidence and gives them a sense of purpose.

Using relationship skills to form positive connections with other people is never a waste. When people learn to work together better, they have a better chance of accomplishing almost any goal. Successful relationship skills pave the way for success in school, the workplace, and people's personal lives.

GLOSSARY

ally

a person who supports and encourages people in his or her community

biases

beliefs that favor one way of thinking over another

empathy

the act of considering a situation from another person's viewpoint

hijab

a head covering that some Muslim women wear in public

rally

to gather in support of someone or something

stereotypes

oversimplified beliefs about a group of people

sustained

kept up or continued over time

SOURCE NOTES

CHAPTER ONE: RELATIONSHIP SKILLS AT SCHOOL

1. Danny Wagner, "Resources to Integrate Teamwork into Every Classroom Every Day," *Common Sense Education*, April 25, 2019. www.commonsense.org.

2. Quoted in "An Interview on Student Success & Wellbeing," *Pegasus Springs Education Collective*, June 12, 2019. www.pegasussprings.org.

CHAPTER TWO: RELATIONSHIP SKILLS AT HOME

3. Jodi Dworkin and Joyce Serido, "The Role of Families in Supporting Social and Emotional Learning," *University of Minnesota Extension*, February 2017. https://conservancy.umn.edu.

4. Juliann Garey, "Teaching Kids How to Deal with Conflict," *Child Mind Institute*, n.d. https://childmind.org.

CHAPTER THREE: RELATIONSHIP SKILLS WITH FRIENDS

5. Vincent Iannelli, "How Kids Make and Keep Friends," *Verywell Family*, July 21, 2021. www.verywellfamily.com.

6. Michelle Garcia Winner and Pamela Crooke, "10 Truths & Tips for Making and Keeping Friends," *Social Thinking*, November 17, 2020. www.socialthinking.com.

CHAPTER FOUR: RELATIONSHIP SKILLS IN THE COMMUNITY

7. Danny Wagner, "4 Tools to Help Kids Develop Empathy and Cultural Humility," *KQED*, November 3, 2017. www.kqed.org.

8. Cassandra Kiger, "Why Is Social Emotional Learning Important?" *Affinity Mentoring*, October 4, 2021. https://affinitymentoring.org.

FOR FURTHER RESEARCH

BOOKS

Alexis Burling, *Healthy Romantic Relationships*. Minneapolis, MN: Abdo Publishing, 2021.

Walt K. Moon, *Volunteering for the Homeless*. San Diego, CA: BrightPoint Press, 2022.

Erin Nicks, *Developing Social Awareness*. San Diego, CA: BrightPoint Press, 2023.

INTERNET SOURCES

Aaron Heldt, "The Importance of Community Service in a Teen's Life," *Bridge Teen Center*, February 17, 2021. https://thebridgeteencenter.org.

Julie Jargon, "Social and Emotional Learning Has Never Been More Important," *Wall Street Journal*, September 15, 2020. www.wsj.com.

Jill Suttie, "36 Questions That Can Help Kids Make Friends," *Greater Good Magazine*, July 27, 2021. https://greatergood.berkeley.edu.

WEBSITES

Collaborative for Academic, Social, and Emotional Learning
www.casel.org

CASEL stands for the Collaborative for Academic, Social, and Emotional Learning. This nonprofit organization partners with schools and communities to educate and promote this education practice.

Committee for Children
www.cfchildren.org

This global nonprofit organization champions the well-being of kids through social-emotional learning.

Understood.org
www.understood.org

Understood is a nonprofit organization and website that provides free resources and support for people who have difficulties with attention, learning, and social skills.

INDEX

ally, 65
assumptions, 48–50

box breathing, 43
bullying, 24, 52

common interests, 54–55
communication, 34, 38, 41, 43, 49, 55–59
cultural humility, 18, 68–69, 71

discrimination, 66
Dworkin, Jodi, 34

empathy, 11, 24, 43, 54

Freedom Writers, 20

Garey, Juliann, 39–40

hijab, 44, 49, 50

Iannelli, Vincent, 55

Kiger, Cassandra, 70

listening, 24, 26, 36, 38, 43, 59

negative social pressure, 65–66

perspectives, 52, 59

Serido, Joyce, 34
stereotypes, 15, 69

teamwork, 16
Trevor Project, 64

volunteering, 70–71, 72, 73

Wagner, Danny, 18, 68
Walsh, Erin, 25–26
Winner, Michelle Garcia, 57–58

IMAGE CREDITS

Cover: © Odua Images/Shutterstock Images
5: © Eduard Figueres/iStockphoto
7: © Johnny Greig/iStockphoto
8: © SDI Productions/iStockphoto
10: © People Images/iStockphoto
13: © Kan Chana/Shutterstock Images
15: © Sam Edwards/iStockphoto
17: © Daniel M. Ernst/Shutterstock Images
19: © Fang Xia Nuo/iStockphoto
23: © Monkey Business Images/Shutterstock Images
27: © Monkey Business Images/Shutterstock Images
29: © Dejan Dundjerski/Shutterstock Images
31: © Pixel Shot/Shutterstock Images
33: © Monkey Business Images/Shutterstock Images
35: © Light Field Studios/Shutterstock Images
39: © Kazuma Seki/iStockphoto
41: © Aldo Murillo/iStockphoto
42: © Aldo Murillo/iStockphoto
45: © Dimensions/iStockphoto
47: © Daniel M. Ernst/Shutterstock Images
49: © Fizkes/Shutterstock Images
50: © Martine Doucet/iStockphoto
53: © Kate Sept. 2004/iStockphoto
54: © Omg Images/iStockphoto
57: © SDI Productions/iStockphoto
61: © Alessandro Biascioli/iStockphoto
62: © Fizkes/Shutterstock Images
67: © Constantinis/iStockphoto
69: © Fat Camera/iStockphoto
72: © Macro Vector/Shutterstock Images

ABOUT THE AUTHOR

Tammy Gagne has written dozens of books for both adults and children. Her recent titles include *The History of Racism in America* and *Race and the Media in Modern America*. She lives in northern New England with her husband and son.